WILD WEATHER

TORNADOES

by Cody Crane

Children's Press®
An imprint of Scholastic Inc.

Scientific Consultant
Adam Sobel
Columbia University
New York, New York

Reading Consultant
Maggie Peterson
Julia A. Stark Elementary School
Stamford, Connecticut

Copyright © 2025 by Scholastic Inc.

All rights reserved. Published by Children's Press, an imprint of Scholastic Inc., *Publishers since 1920.* SCHOLASTIC, CHILDREN'S PRESS, and associated logos are trademarks and/or registered trademarks of Scholastic Inc.

The publisher does not have any control over and does not assume any responsibility for author or third-party websites or their content.

No part of this publication may be reproduced, stored in a retrieval system, or transmitted in any form or by any means, electronic, mechanical, photocopying, recording, or otherwise, or used to train any artificial intelligence technologies, without written permission of the publisher. For information regarding permission, write to Scholastic Inc., Attention: Permissions Department, 557 Broadway, New York, NY 10012.

Library of Congress Cataloging-in-Publication Data available

ISBN 978-1-5461-3593-7 (library binding) / ISBN 978-1-5461-3594-4 (paperback)

10 9 8 7 6 5 4 3 2 1   25 26 27 28 29

Printed in China 62
First edition, 2025

Series produced by Spooky Cheetah Press
Book design by Kathleen Petelinsek

Photos ©: Theriault/Getty Images; 6–7: MJ Gillespie Photography; 8–9: JasonWeingart/Wikimedia; 10–11: Jim McMahon/Mapman®; 14–15: Marko Korosec/Solent News/Shutterstock; 18–19: Ryan McGinnis/Alamy Images; 21: Courtesy NWS/NOAA; 22–23 background: Danny Johnston/AP Images; 24: NOAA/Flickr; 25 top: NOAA; 25 center: Wikimedia; 25 bottom: Vladimir Razguliaev/Alamy Images; 27 top: GabrielPevide/Getty Images; 28 bottom: Jeffrey Isaac Greenberg 12+/Alamy Images; 29 top: Education Images/UIG/Getty Images; 30 center: nycshooter/Getty Images; 30 bottom: JEWEL SAMAD/AFP/Getty Images.

All other photos © Shutterstock.

TABLE OF CONTENTS

Introduction ... 4

CHAPTER 1
What Is a Tornado? ... 6

CHAPTER 2
How Do Tornadoes Form? ... 14

CHAPTER 3
Predicting Tornadoes ... 20

If a Tornado Happens ... 28
Glossary ... 31
Index ... 32
About the Author ... 32

Introduction

Thunder rumbles outside. The sky gets very dark. The wind sounds like a train. A tornado is coming. Tornadoes are dangerous. It is not safe to go outside. It is not safe to even watch the storm from a window.

A tornado starts from a funnel cloud. Can you guess why it is called that?

Tornadoes are also known as twisters.

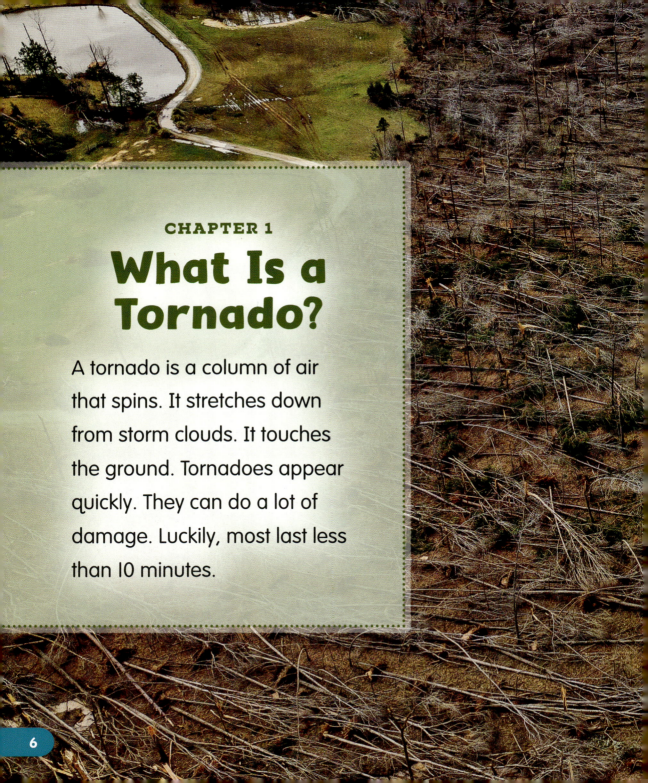

CHAPTER 1

What Is a Tornado?

A tornado is a column of air that spins. It stretches down from storm clouds. It touches the ground. Tornadoes appear quickly. They can do a lot of damage. Luckily, most last less than 10 minutes.

Tornadoes can happen any time of year.

A tornado knocked down all these trees. But this stronger house was left standing.

Tornadoes do not stay put. They move across the land. Some move as fast as a speeding car. Others move slowly. Some move in a straight line. Others change direction.

These seven photos show how a tornado moves across the land.

Tornadoes are always spinning as they move across the land.

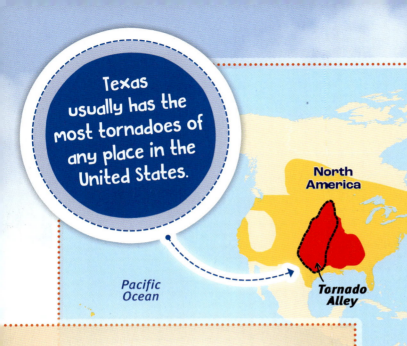

Texas usually has the most tornadoes of any place in the United States.

Tornadoes happen in many parts of the world. But most occur in the United States. Every year there are more than 1,000 tornadoes there. Many happen in an area called Tornado Alley. It stretches across a flat area. It is in the middle of the country.

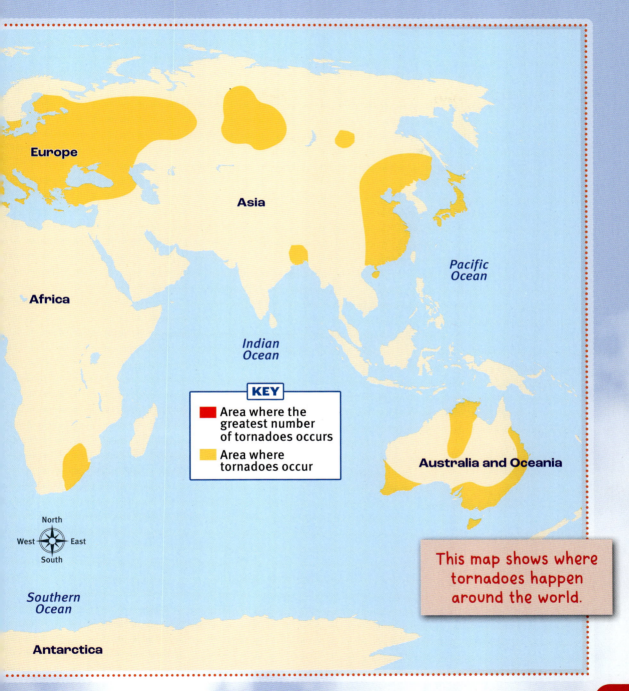

Scientists have made a discovery. They noticed that tornado patterns are changing. For example, in the United States, fewer tornadoes are touching down in the center of the country.

More than one tornado can come from a single storm. These tornadoes are called a tornado family.

But more tornadoes are happening in the southern and eastern parts of the country. That could be because of **climate change**. Or tornado patterns may naturally shift over time.

This is a photo of a tornado family.

CHAPTER 2

How Do Tornadoes Form?

Most tornadoes form from supercells. Supercells are rare thunderstorms that spin. Supercells form when cool, dry air meets warm, wet air. The two types of air swirl together. That creates strong winds. They can form tornadoes.

This is a photo of a supercell.

A supercell kicks up dust as it spins. That can make the sky orange.

15

This diagram shows how a tornado forms from a supercell.

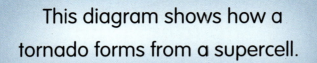

1

Warm air rises and cool air sinks inside the storm. That creates strong winds.

2

The winds push in different directions. That causes the center of the storm to spin.

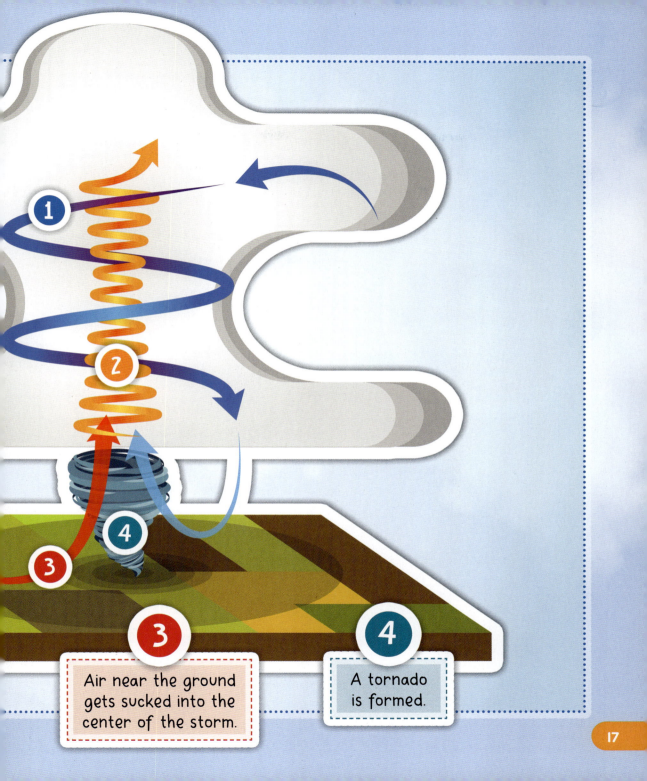

3 Air near the ground gets sucked into the center of the storm.

4 A tornado is formed.

17

A tornado can also form from a squall line. That is a group of thunderstorms. They sweep quickly over an area. These storms bring heavy rains and strong winds.

A squall line is a group of thunderstorms arranged in a long, skinny line.

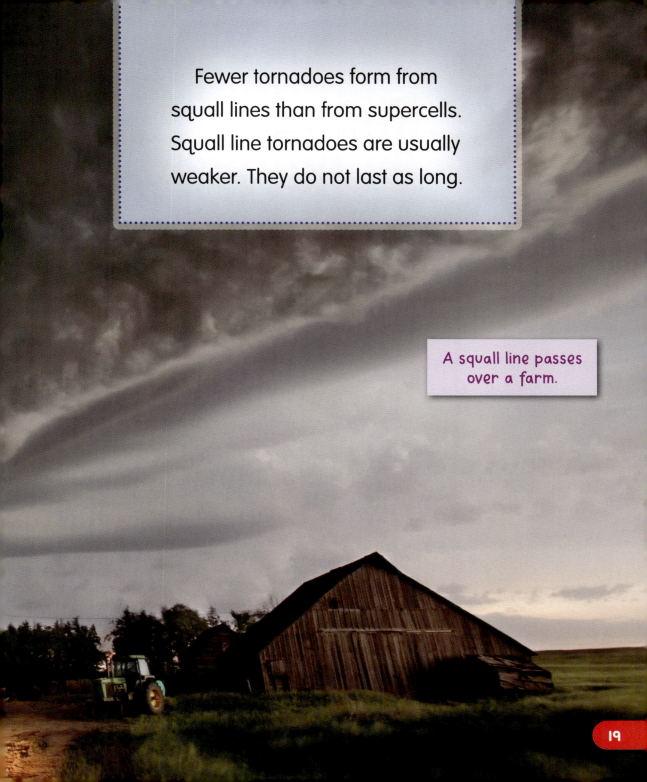

Fewer tornadoes form from squall lines than from supercells. Squall line tornadoes are usually weaker. They do not last as long.

A squall line passes over a farm.

CHAPTER 3

Predicting Tornadoes

Meteorologists are scientists who **predict** weather. They watch storms that can cause tornadoes. They use tools like **radar**. Radar shows storms from above. Meteorologists may think a tornado will form. They warn people to keep them safe. They put out two types of alerts: Tornado Watch and Tornado Warning.

TYPE OF ALERT	MEANING
Tornado Watch	Weather could cause a tornado. Get ready to take shelter.
Tornado Warning	A tornado has been spotted. Take shelter now.

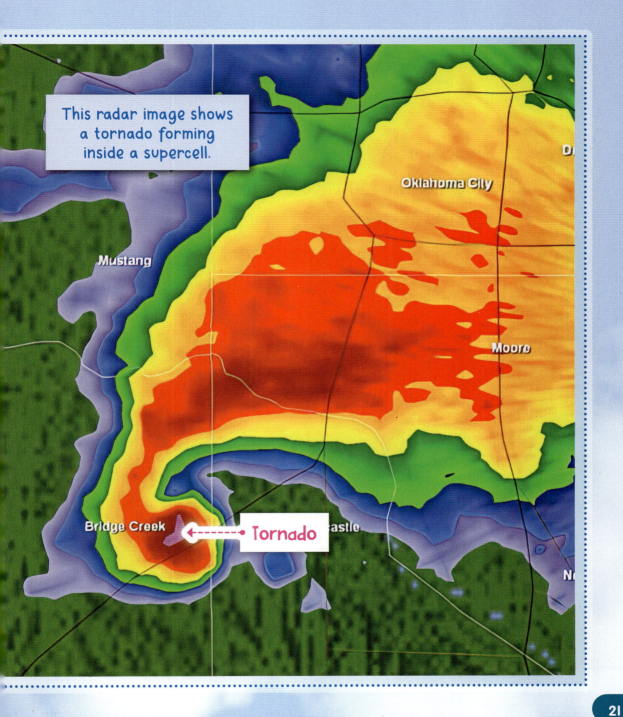

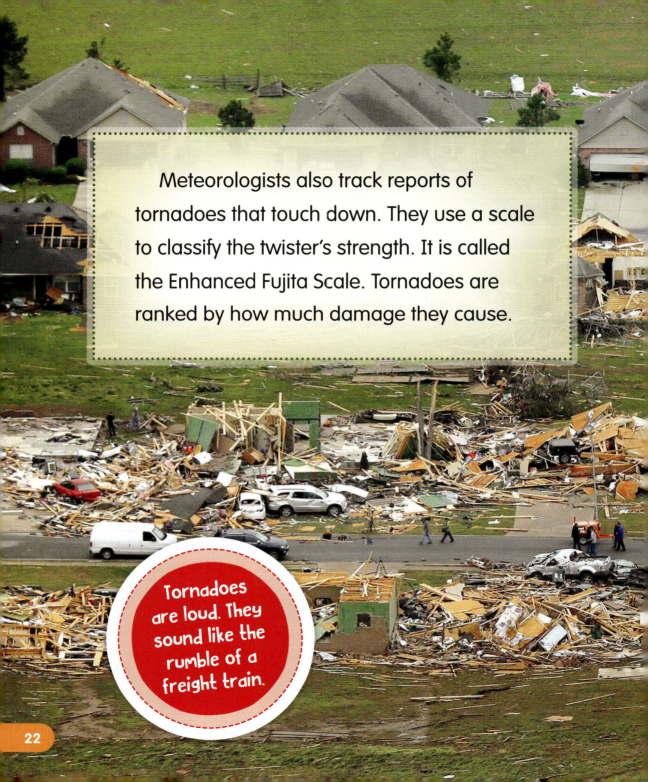

Meteorologists also track reports of tornadoes that touch down. They use a scale to classify the twister's strength. It is called the Enhanced Fujita Scale. Tornadoes are ranked by how much damage they cause.

Tornadoes are loud. They sound like the rumble of a freight train.

ENHANCED FUJITA SCALE

Tornado Rating | **Wind Speed and Damage Level**

0
65–85 mph (105–137 kph)
Light: some tree branches broken

1
86–110 mph (138–177 kph)
Moderate: windows broken, roofs damaged

2
111–135 mph (178–217 kph)
Strong: roofs torn off houses, trees uprooted

3
136–165 mph (218–266 kph)
Severe: walls of homes knocked down

4
166–200 mph (267–322 kph)
Devastating: homes flattened, cars flipped

5
201 mph (323 kph) or greater
Incredible: damage to even the sturdiest steel and concrete buildings

Scientists want to learn more about why tornadoes form. They use special tools to study storms that can create tornadoes. Take a look at some of them here! These tools measure wind speeds, temperature, and **humidity**. Humidity is the amount of moisture in the air. They also measure **air pressure**, or how heavy the air is.

Some scientists who study tornadoes are called storm chasers.

This heavy-duty truck can follow storms safely.

Meteorologists are getting better at knowing when tornadoes will happen. They can warn people to prepare. Tornadoes do not happen often. And they do not last long. The sky will clear. Then it is safe to head back outside!

A rainbow may appear after a storm.

IF A TORNADO HAPPENS

Tornadoes can happen in many places. Talk to the grown-ups in your house about these steps for staying safe in case of a tornado.

Listen Up
Check weather reports when there is a severe thunderstorm.

Get Alerts
There are emergency weather alerts for your area. Have an adult sign up to get these texts, emails, or phone calls.

Know Where to Go
Choose a room in your home to meet if there is a tornado. The safest place is a basement or storm cellar. Or find an inside room with no windows on the lowest floor.

Practice a Safety Drill
Practice getting to your chosen safe place. If a tornado is approaching, move immediately to the designated safe place.

(Turn the page.)

Seek Shelter
If you do not have a safe place in your home, do not stay there. Instead, go to the nearest storm shelter. Or look nearby for a sturdy building, like a hospital or mall.

Take Cover
Stay in your safe place until you are told you can leave.

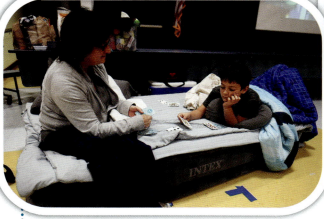

Steer Clear
After the tornado, be careful of fallen trees, power lines, and other **debris**.

GLOSSARY

air pressure (AIR PRESH-ur) the weight of the air, which is greater near the earth than it is high up

climate change (KLYE-mit CHAYNJ) global warming and other changes in the weather and weather patterns that are happening because of human activity

debris (duh-BREE) the pieces of something that has been broken or destroyed

drone (DROHN) an aircraft without a pilot that is controlled remotely

humidity (hyoo-MID-i-tee) the amount of moisture in the air

meteorologists (mee-tee-uh-RAH-luh-jists) experts who study weather

predict (pri-DIKT) to say what will happen in the future

radar (RAY-dahr) a device used in weather forecasting to detect rain and wind

INDEX

Page numbers in **bold** indicate illustrations.

air pressure 24
climate change 13
drone 25, **25**
Enhanced Fujita Scale 22, 23
funnel **4–5**, 5
humidity 24
meteorologists 20, 22, 26
plane 25, **25**
radar 20, **21**, 25
squall line 18–19, **18–19**

staying safe 4, 28–30, **28–30**
storm chasers 24
supercell 14–15, **14–15**, 16–17, **16–17**, 19, 21
temperature 24
thunder 4
tornado alerts 20
Tornado Alley 10
tornado destruction 6–7, 7, **22–23**
tornado duration 6, 19, 26

tornado family 12, **12–13**
tornado formation 14–19, **14–19**
tornado movement 8–9, **8–9**
tornado patterns 12–13
truck 24, **24**
weather balloon 25, **25**
where tornadoes occur 10, **10–11**
wind 4, 16, 18, 24

ABOUT THE AUTHOR

Cody Crane loves writing books for children. She and her family live near Tornado Alley. Luckily, they have never experienced one!